Dora's Sleepover

by Lara Bergen
illustrated by Victoria Miller

Ready-to-Read

Simon Spotlight/Nick Jr.
New York   London   Toronto   Sydney

visit us at www.abdopublishing.com

Reinforced library bound edition published in 2009 by Spotlight, a division of ABDO Publishing Group, 8000 West 78th Street, Edina, Minnesota 55439. Published by agreement with Simon Spotlight, an imprint of Simon & Schuster Children's Publishing Division.

SIMON SPOTLIGHT

An imprint of Simon & Schuster Children's Publishing Division
1230 Avenue of the Americas, New York, NY 10020
Copyright © 2006 Viacom International Inc. Based on the TV series *Dora the Explorer*® as seen on Nick Jr.® NICK JR., *Dora the Explorer*, and all related titles, logos, and characters are trademarks of Viacom International Inc.

Library of Congress Cataloging-in-Publication Data

This title was previously cataloged with the following information:

Bergen, Lara.
 Dora's sleepover / by Lara Bergen ; illustrated by Victoria Miller.
 p. cm. -- (Ready-to-read. Level 1; #12)
 "Based on the TV series Dora the Explorer as seen on Nick Jr."
 I. Miller, Victoria (Victoria H.) II. Dora the explorer (Television program). III. Title.
IV. Series. V. Series: Dora the explorer
PZ7.B44985 Dor 2006
[E]--dc22   2006014520

ISBN-13: 978-1-59961-438-0 (reinforced library bound edition)
ISBN-10: 1-59961-438-3 (reinforced library bound edition)

Spotlight

All Spotlight books have reinforced library binding
and are manufactured in the United States of America.

Hi! I am .

It is a big night!

I am having a sleepover
with my best friend, ,

at his !

First I need to pack  .

Do you see what I should

pack?

I will take my ,
PAJAMAS

my , my ,
FLASHLIGHT SLEEPING BAG

and my of stories.
BOOK PIRATE

loves stories!

BOOTS PIRATE

MAMI has made some 🍪 COOKIES

for 🐵 BOOTS and me. Yum!

MAMI puts the 🍪 COOKIES

in a 🧺 BASKET.

Do **you** like ?
COOKIES

Thank you, .
MAMI

Good-bye!

How do we get
to 's  ?
BOOTS   TREE HOUSE
 can show us
MAP
the way.

We go through the ,
TUNNEL

then through the ,
JUNGLE

and that's how we get to

's .

BOOTS   TREE HOUSE

We made it to the  .
TUNNEL

But the  is **so** dark!
TUNNEL

Is there something

in my  that will
BACKPACK

help us see in the dark?

Yeah! A FLASHLIGHT !

We made it through the .
TUNNEL

Now we need to go

through the .
JUNGLE

Uh-oh! Do you see

someone behind that ?
TREE

It is  !

SWIPER

 wants to swipe our

SWIPER

 of 🍪 .

BASKET   COOKIES

Say " 🦝 , no swiping!"

SWIPER

We stopped 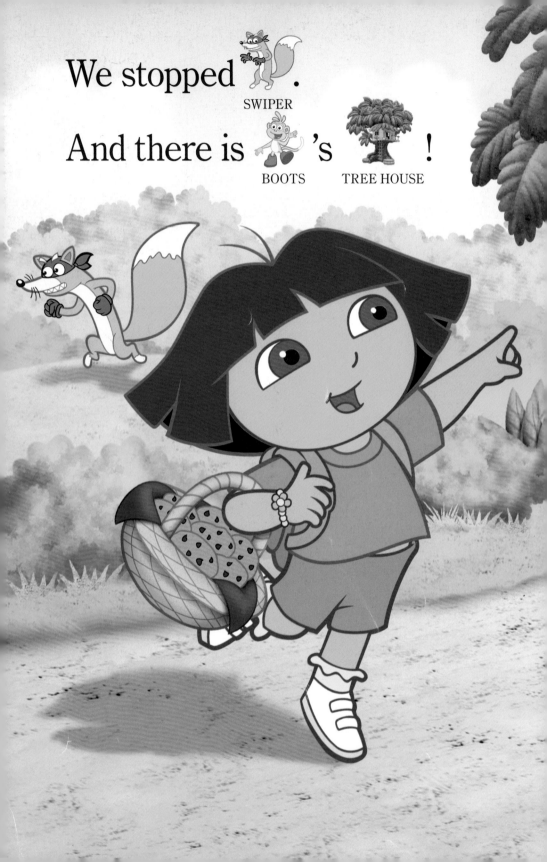.
SWIPER

And there is 's !
BOOTS TREE HOUSE

We can climb the
LADDER

to get to 's .
BOOTS   TREE HOUSE

Hi,  ! I am ready

for our sleepover!

I have my  ,
PAJAMAS

my FLASHLIGHT , my SLEEPING BAG ,

my BOOK of PIRATE stories,

and a BASKET of COOKIES

from MAMI !

It is time to put on our .
PAJAMAS

Then we can turn on our

 and eat the .
FLASHLIGHTS COOKIES

Yum!

I can read my  BOOK

of stories

PIRATE

to too.

BOOTS

Look at the 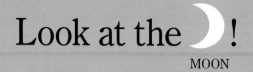!

MOON

The is so big and bright.

MOON

 yawns.

BOOTS

 is sleepy.

BOOTS

I am sleepy too.

We get into our .

SLEEPING BAGS

Good night, 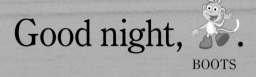.

And good night

to you, too!